Hiya! My name Thudd. Best robot friend of Drewd. Thudd know lotsa stuff. What kind of plant eat meat. What part of jungle ant taste good.

Drewd like to invent stuff. Thudd help! But Drewd make lotsa mistakes. Drewd invent shrinking machine. Now Drewd small as beetle. Fly into jungle on back of bird. Thudd worried. Want to see what happen? Turn page, please!

Get lost with
Andrew, Judy, and Thudd
in all their exciting adventures!

ANDREW LOST

BY J. C. GREENBURG

ILLUSTRATED
BY JAN GERARDI

15

IN THE JUNGLE

A STEPPING STONE BOOK™

Random House 🏠 New York

To Dan, Zack, and the real Andrew,
with a galaxy of love.
To the children who read these books: I wish
you wonderful questions. Questions are
telescopes into the universe!
—J.C.G.

To Cathy Goldsmith, with many thanks.
—J.G.

Text copyright © 2007 by J. C. Greenburg
Illustrations copyright © 2007 by Jan Gerardi

All rights reserved. Published in the United States by Random House
Children's Books, a division of Random House, Inc., New York.

RANDOM HOUSE and colophon are registered trademarks and A STEPPING
STONE BOOK and colophon are trademarks of Random House, Inc.
ANDREW LOST is a trademark of J. C. Greenburg.

www.randomhouse.com/kids/AndrewLost
www.AndrewLost.com

Educators and librarians, for a variety of teaching tools, visit us at
www.randomhouse.com/teachers

Library of Congress Cataloging-in-Publication Data
Greenburg, J. C. (Judith C.)
In the jungle / by J. C. Greenburg ; illustrated by Jan Gerardi. —
1st ed.
    p.   cm. — (Andrew Lost ; 15) "A Stepping Stone Book."
SUMMARY: Lost in an Australian rain forest, Andrew, Judy, and Thudd
the robot, who are still the size of insects, must evade rhinoceros
beetles, tarantulas, flesh-eating plants, and a host of other threats as
they make their way toward the village where Uncle Al will meet
them.
ISBN 978-0-375-83564-3 (trade) — ISBN 978-0-375-93564-0 (lib. bdg.)
[1. Rain forests—Fiction. 2. Robots—Fiction. 3. Cousins—Fiction.
4. Australia—Fiction.] I. Gerardi, Jan, ill. II. Title. III. Series:
Greenburg, J. C. (Judith C.). Andrew Lost ; 15.
PZ7.G82785Iot 2005   [Fic]—dc22   2006003446

Printed in the United States of America
10 9   First Edition

CONTENTS

ANDREW'S WORLD

Andrew Dubble

Andrew is ten years old, but he's been inventing things since he was four. Andrew's inventions usually get him into trouble, like the time he accidentally took the Water Bug underwater vehicle on a trip to the deepest place on earth.

Andrew's newest invention was supposed to save the world from getting buried in garbage. Instead, it squashed Andrew and his cousin Judy down to beetle size. They got hauled off to a dump, thrown up by a seagull, and carried off by a bat. Now they're flying across the Pacific Ocean on the back of a bird!

Judy Dubble

Judy is Andrew's thirteen-year-old cousin. She's been snuffled into a dog's nose, pooped out of a whale, and had her pajamas chewed by a Tyrannosaurus—all because of Andrew. Judy thought that nothing weirder could ever happen to her—until today.

Thudd

The **H**andy **U**ltra-**D**igital **D**etective. Thudd is a super-smart robot and Andrew's best friend. He has helped save Andrew and Judy from the exploding sun, the giant squid, and a monster asteroid. Now can he protect his tiny buddies from meat-eating plants, dinner-plate-sized spiders, and shocking animals?

The Goa Constrictor

This giant fake snake is Andrew's newest invention. *Goa* is sort of short for **G**arbage

Goes **A**way. The Goa is supposed to keep the world from getting buried in garbage by squashing rotting vegetables, green meat, and dirty diapers down to teensy-weensy specks. Unfortunately for Andrew and Judy, the Goa doesn't just shrink garbage. In two minutes and one stinky burp, the Goa can shrink anything—and anyone!

Uncle Al

He's a super-secret scientist, Andrew and Judy's uncle, and Thudd's inventor. Uncle Al is really smart, but is he smart enough to save his beetle-sized niece and nephew from the incredibly weird dangers of the Australian jungle? Even the *trees* are deadly!

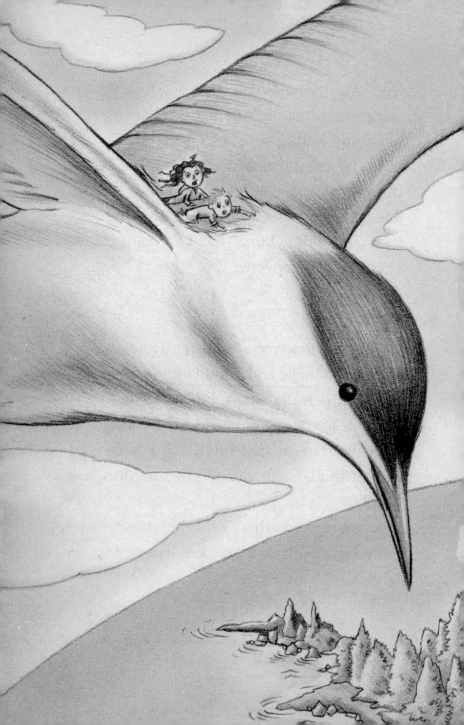

IT'S A JUNGLE DOWN THERE

I wonder where we are now, thought Andrew Dubble. Andrew, no bigger than a beetle, poked his head above a feather on the bird's back. A cold wind smacked his face as he peered at the earth far below.

"Wowzers schnauzers!" Andrew shouted. "I see green down there! It's land! Now maybe this bird will take a break. She's been flying over the ocean for *ages*!"

Another feather on the bird's back twitched. A pile of frizzy dark hair popped up and went wild in the wind. It was Andrew's thirteen-year-old cousin, Judy.

Judy shook her hair away from her face. "Fat chance, Bug-Brain," she yelled above the wind. "This bird is an *arctic tern*! She's on her way to Antarctica! Unless Uncle Al gets our messages, we're penguin chow!"

Uncle Al was Andrew and Judy's uncle, and he was also a super-smart, super-secret scientist.

meep . . . "Unkie Al not call back yet," came a squeaky voice from Andrew's shirt pocket. It was Andrew's little silver mini-robot and best friend, Thudd. "And penguin not eat bugs."

"Oh, great," groaned Judy. "So we'll just turn into bug-sized ice cubes."

The bird spread her wings wide and glided.

"She's going lower," said Andrew.

Now Andrew could see a wide, sandy beach and a forest beyond.

"Looks like a deserted island," said Andrew.

"Noop! Noop! Noop!" said Thudd. "Australia! Continent!"

"Australia!" said Judy. "Cities! *People!* Someone could find us!"

As the bird glided lower still, Andrew saw driftwood and heaps of seaweed on the beach. But he didn't see any people.

Now the bird was flying over the forest. It looked like a bumpy blanket of green. Here and there, tall trees poked through. A river zigzagged through the greenness like a silver snake.

The bird swooped down through the treetops and into the forest.

At first Andrew could hardly see in the dim light under the leaves. His eyes were used to the brightness of the open sky.

The air was alive with screeches and cries and cackles, chirps and whistles, and a sound like crazy laughter.

The bird dove under huge fan-shaped leaves.

"Look at this place!" Judy said. "Nothing but tangles of trees and vines! It's a *jungle*!"

meep . . . "Rain forest," said Thudd. "Australian rain forest strange, strange, strange!

"Got plants and animals that not live any other place. Got most poisonous snakes in world! People found eighty-six thousand kindsa insects! Found ten thousand kindsa spiders!

"People always finding new kindsa plants and animals. Maybe Drewd and Oody find new stuff."

"Neato mosquito!" said Andrew. "Maybe I'll find a new kind of spider."

"Eeeuw!" Judy groaned. "Ten thousand kinds of spiders are way too many!"

meep . . . "Maybe Oody find new kinda plant," said Thudd. "Rain forest got lotsa plants. Make lotsa oxygen for earth. Lotsa medicines come from rain-forest plants."

Judy rolled her eyes. "We don't need to find *plants*," she said. "We need to find *people*."

meep . . . "Rain forest not got lotsa people," said Thudd.

The bird slowed down. She settled herself on a branch midway up a tall tree.

The air felt warm and damp against Andrew's skin.

Andrew sniffed in the jungle smells—green leaves, sweet flowers, and something musty, like a wet basement.

Andrew looked down to the floor of the rain forest way below. "We must be six stories above the ground," he said. "But at least we're on land again."

"Let's get off this bird chop-chop," said Judy, "before she heads for penguin country."

Andrew climbed down through the feathers on the tern's back. He reached a long flight feather at the edge of a wing.

"Hmmmm . . . ," he pondered. "We can jump from this feather to the branch below."

Just then, the bird swiveled her head.

Andrew saw his reflection in a shiny black eye. "Um, I wonder what arctic terns eat," he said.

meep . . . "Eat little fish. Shrimp. Insects, too," said Thudd.

"Or insect-sized humans," said Andrew. He ducked under a flight feather and pulled it down tightly over himself.

A pointy red beak dove into the feathers behind Andrew. Then it plunged into the feathers close to Andrew. The beak grabbed the bottom of one of the feathers. It nibbled along the edges right up to the tip.

meep . . . "Bird preen feather," said Thudd. "Spread oil to keep feather dry. Preening make feather smooth for flying. Get rid of little bugs, too."

The beak preened another feather even closer to Andrew.

"Wowzers schnauzers!" said Andrew. "We've got to get out of here!"

Just then, the red beak grabbed the feather he was clinging to and began to preen it. The beak pushed Andrew to the very tip of the feather. He was barely hanging on. That black eye was looking right at him.

She's hungry and I'm a bug, thought Andrew. He let go.

2

SSSSSSS . . .
KEEKEEKEE
KEEKEEKEE

"Yaaaargh!" hollered Andrew, tumbling down and down. He waved his hands, frantically trying to grab a leaf or a vine.

Finally, he snagged something with his right hand.

"Wowzers schnauzers!" cried Andrew. He was clutching a tall blade of grass. The forest floor was inches below.

But he was dangling above something strange. It looked like a red-and-white tub covered with hairs. It was so big that beetle-sized Andrew could have taken a bath in it.

"Holy moly!" said Andrew. "What's *that*?"

meep . . . "Pitcher plant!" said Thudd. "Pitcher plant carnivorous. Eat meat.

"Got special juice at bottom of pitcher. Juice digest bug meat that fall inside plant. Like stomach digest pizza inside Drewd."

"Jumping gerbils!" said Andrew. "A meat-eating plant, and I'm meat!" He began walking his hands along the blade of grass to get away from the pitcher plant.

Suddenly the blade bent. Andrew dipped lower. One of Andrew's legs slipped inside the pitcher!

Uh-oh, thought Andrew. He tried to pull his leg out, but the inside of the pitcher was too smooth and slippery. Andrew was sweating. The screeching, cackling jungle noises made it hard to think.

With his free leg, Andrew gave a mighty push against the outside of the pitcher plant. He got his other leg out!

"Whew!" he sighed, still dangling from

the grass. His ears picked up a new sound nearby.

Sssssss . . . keekeekee . . . keekeekee . . .

On the ground beside the pitcher plant, two gigantic black beetles were creeping toward each other. They were hissing and clicking. At the front of each beetle's head was a curved horn as long as the rest of its body.

"Holy moly!" whispered Andrew. "Those guys look as big as trucks!"

meep . . . "Rhinoceros beetles!" said Thudd.

Now the beetles' enormous horns were almost touching. They stopped. They stamped

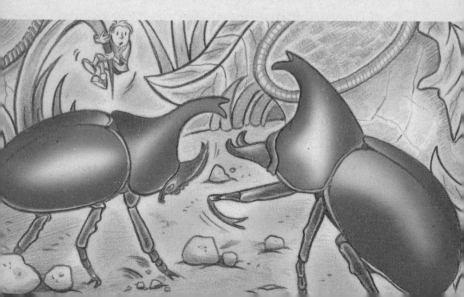

their clawed feet and wagged their armored heads.

One beetle charged the other. They locked horns under Andrew's blade of grass. They shook their giant heads from side to side. The bigger beetle flipped the smaller one on its back. The feet of the smaller beetle clawed at the bigger beetle's head.

meep . . . "Male rhinoceros beetles fight to get mate," said Thudd. "Horn strong, strong, strong! Can cut off head of other rhinoceros beetle!"

"Watch out below!" came a yell from above.

Andrew looked up to see Judy tumbling through the air.

"Ooomph!" Judy landed on a taller blade of grass right next to Andrew. Her feet smacked the top of Andrew's head.

"Youch!" he hollered.

His stem bent lower. His feet clunked against the horn of the bigger beetle!

Sssssssss . . . hissed the beetle. It reared up on its back legs. Its front legs clawed the air. The tip of its terrible horn touched Andrew's nose!

"YAAAAARGH!" screamed Andrew.

"Andrew!" shouted Judy. "There's a bright green twig sticking out from the tree trunk behind you. Grab it!"

Andrew swung himself toward the tree. He spotted the twig and wrapped his legs quickly around it.

"Make room for me," yelled Judy, swinging herself at the twig. She slammed into it and scrambled on behind Andrew.

"Now climb a little way up the tree trunk," said Judy. "Before we fall into the middle of this stupid beetle battle. Then we've got to call Uncle Al again."

Andrew felt a jolt. "Um, maybe we don't have to climb up the tree trunk," said Andrew. "This *twig* is climbing."

THE CASE OF THE KILLER TREE

3

THUDD

"Cheese Louise!" exclaimed Judy. "It *is* climbing!"

meep . . . "Drewd and Oody getting ride on stick insect," said Thudd. "Rain forest got lotsa insects that look like stick, look like twig. Got insects that look like leaf, too."

"Weird-a-mundo!" said Judy, jiggling on the back of the skittering bug.

meep . . . "Good disguise for prey animal," said Thudd. "Look like stuff around it. Disguise called camouflage. Hard for predator animal to find prey animal that got camouflage."

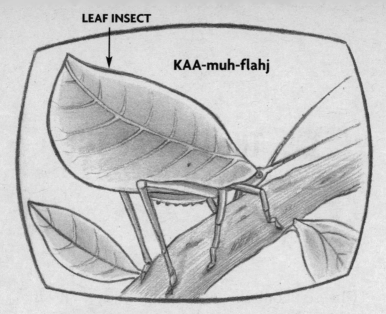

LEAF INSECT

KAA-muh-flahj

"Camouflage, shamouflage," said Judy. "We could get bounced off this bug any minute. Call Uncle Al again, Thudd."

"Okey-dokey," said Thudd.

There were three rows of buttons on Thudd's chest. All of them glowed green, except the big purple button in the middle. Thudd pressed the purple button. It blinked three times and went dark.

meep . . . "Unkie not answer," said Thudd.

"He's probably on some super-secret project," said Andrew.

Judy groaned. "Let's get off this stupid

bug as soon as it stops," she said. "We'll look for a safe place and wait till Uncle Al calls us."

As the stick insect skittered up the tree, Andrew noticed that the tree trunk looked like a tangle of fat snakes.

"This is a super-strange tree," said Andrew.

meep . . . "Strangler fig tree," said Thudd.

"Strangler!" said Judy.

meep . . . "Fig tree gotta strangle other tree to grow," said Thudd.

"Start when bird eat strangler fig fruit. Bird fly. Bird poop. Fig seed fall into treetop. Seed sprout. Roots grow down to ground. Get big, big, big! Strangle tree underneath. Roots turn into trunk for strangler fig."

"Wowzers schnauzers!" said Andrew.

"Meat-eating plants! Killer trees!"

"Weird-a-mundo!" said Judy.

All of a sudden, part of the gray-brown tree trunk above them seemed to whip around. It was scrambling toward them!

Andrew squinted. He made out a lizardy head with fearsome spikes at the top. A row of spikes ran down its neck.

"Yaaaah!" screamed Judy.

"Holy moly!" yelled Andrew.

Eek! squeaked Thudd. "Forest dragon lizard! Eat stick insects!"

The creature's neck was puffing out. Its mouth opened—a pink-purple cave surrounded by small, sharp teeth.

Their stick insect turned away from the forest dragon. Then it was still as a statue.

Judy gave it a little kick. "Get going! Giddyap! That monster is going to *eat* you!"

But the bug didn't move. Suddenly Andrew was getting soaked. His eyes were burning. His nose filled with a peppermint smell so strong, it hurt to breathe.

"Blurf!" yelped Andrew.

"Aaaack!" hollered Judy. An awful spray was shooting from the back of the insect's head—and blasting the lizard's face!

The lizard shook its head. In an instant, it sped down the tree trunk.

The stick insect scurried higher up the tree trunk.

"Eck-uh! ECK-UH!" Judy coughed. "It smells like peppermint, but it's *awful!*"

meep . . . "This bug called peppermint-stick insect," said Thudd. "Peppermint smell make lotsa predators go way!"

Just then, the big purple button in the middle of Thudd's chest started to blink.

meep . . . "Unkie!" said Thudd.

"Finally!" said Judy.

Thudd's purple button popped open and a beam of purple light zoomed out. At the end of the beam floated a see-through purplish Uncle Al.

Uncle Al's shaggy hair always looked like he had just pulled a sweater over his head. His face crinkled into a smile. "Hey there!" he said with a wave.

"Hey, Uncle Al!" said Andrew.

"I'm away from my laboratory at the moment," continued Uncle Al.

"Oh no!" said Judy. "It's not Uncle Al. It's just his answering machine!"

"Your message has reached my Hologram Helper answering machine," said Uncle Al. "If you're calling to have a friendly chat, please press one. If you have discovered life on another planet, please press two. If you're complaining about smells coming from my laboratory, press three. If this is a purple-button emergency, I will contact you as soon as I can."

The Uncle Al hologram waved. "Goodbye! Have fun! Think big!" Then it disappeared.

NO LAUGHING MATTER

"Cheese Louise!" said Judy. "Just when we need Uncle Al, he's not there!"

Andrew tightened his grip on the peppermint-stick insect. "For now, I guess we should stick with this bug," he said. "At least it's got a way to defend itself, and us too."

As the stick insect climbed higher, the tree trunk became a forest. Mosses grew in velvety green patches and hung in gray strands. Fern fronds leaned over Andrew and Judy like lacy green umbrellas.

As they passed dark holes in the tree trunk, Andrew heard noises—scratching, tapping, hissing.

Andrew imagined what was living deep inside the tree. He shivered.

Ha! Ha! Ha! Hee! Hee! Hoo! Hoo! Hoo! came a sound like a wild party from the treetops.

meep . . . "Laughing kookaburra bird!" said Thudd, pointing way above.

A bird the size of a seagull landed on a branch nearby.

"Jumping gerbils!" said Andrew. "It looks as big as a pterodactyl!"

Then another kookaburra flew down, and then another.

"I'll bet they're looking for bugs," said Judy.

The peppermint-stick insect scuttled onto a branch and was scurrying around a mountain of brown fur.

Ha! Ha! Ha! Hee! Hee! Hoo! Hoo! Hoo!

Andrew turned to see the kookaburras swooping toward them.

Hope this bug has a lot of peppermint spray left, thought Andrew.

The fur mountain next to them shook. In an instant, it unfolded itself into a black-faced, sharp-clawed creature that towered over them like King Kong!

"Yaaaaah!" hollered Judy.

"Uh-oh," Andrew gulped.

meep . . . "Tree kangaroo!" squeaked Thudd. "Kinda kangaroo that always live in trees. Tree kangaroo leap far, far, far! Leap from tree to tree."

The tree kangaroo crouched down, then sprang through the leaves.

Hoo! Hoo! Hoo!

The kookaburras scattered.

The tree kangaroo's jump made the branch dip low, then spring up high and hard.

It's like I'm on a bucking bronco! thought Andrew, trying to hang on to the bug.

But the branch bounced into a dangling vine that scraped Andrew and Judy off the stick insect. They were falling through the branches of the tree!

"Yaaaargh!" hollered Andrew.

"Yiiiiiikes!" screamed Judy.

"Oof!" shouted Andrew, landing on a leaf lower down in the tree.

"Uuuuuck!" came a muffled screech from below. It was Judy. It sounded like she was inside a bottle. "Get me outta here!"

Andrew peered over the edge of the leaf, but he couldn't see Judy.

"Where *are* you?" hollered Andrew.

"Here!" shouted Judy. A hand shot out of a hole in a giant white lump on a tree branch below. The lump was covered with long, sharp thorns taller than Andrew.

"Erk!" yelled Judy. "Hurry up, Bug-Brain! A monster ant is trying to bite off my leg!"

WE JUST ATE WHAT?

"Here I come, Judy!" yelled Andrew.

Grabbing on to ferns and mosses, he lowered himself down the tree trunk.

"Umf! Ack! Ugh!" came the sounds of Judy's struggle.

meep . . . "Oody fall into ant-house plant!" squeaked Thudd. "Ant-house plant got big, fat thorny stem. Ants live inside. Make lotsa tunnels inside stem. Make tunnels for baby ants. Make tunnels for garbage.

"Ants get place to live. Plant get food from ant garbage. Ants happy. Plant happy."

"Judy's sure not happy," said Andrew.

By the time Andrew made his way

through the tall thorns of the ant-house plant, Judy was just pulling herself out of the hole.

"Whew!" she sighed, mopping strands of frizzy hair away from her face.

meep . . . "Drewd and Oody go rest on branch for little bit," said Thudd. "Thudd get treat."

"Treat?" asked Judy. "Everything here is *nasty*."

She and Andrew stepped carefully through the sword-like spines and crept toward the tree trunk.

meep . . . "Put Thudd down, please, Drewd," said Thudd. "Drewd and Oody close eyes."

"Oh, all right," said Judy, finding a velvety patch of moss to stretch out on.

Before long, Thudd came back. He was dragging two leaf pieces. In the middle of each piece was a spot of wetness.

meep . . . "Treat ready!" said Thudd. He

handed a piece of leaf to Andrew and a piece to Judy. "Lick leaf!"

Andrew held the wet spot up to his nose. "Hmmmm . . . ," he mused. "This reminds me of something. Candy. Some kind of candy."

He licked the leaf.

"Super-duper pooper-scooper!" Andrew cheered. "This stuff is *delicious*! Tastes like fizzy lime!"

"What *is* this stuff?" asked Judy, sniffing her leaf.

meep . . . "Oody taste," said Thudd.

"Humph," said Judy. She touched the wet spot with the tip of her tongue.

"YUM!" she said, beaming Thudd a big smile. "Now you have to tell us what it is."

Thudd pinched his way up Andrew's shirt and crept back into his pocket. Then he pointed to a shiny green insect skittering along the branch.

meep . . . "Green ant," said Thudd. "Butt of green ant got powerful lime taste. People in rain forest lick butt of green ant cuz it taste good, good, good!"

Judy's face went white. "Blurgh!" She spit out what was in her mouth, then she kept spitting.

Andrew grinned. "Aw, come on, Judy," he said. "It tasted great, even if it did come from an ant's butt."

Judy wiped her mouth with her sleeve. "If you ever do anything like that again, Thudd, I'm going to take out your batteries and throw them away!"

Suddenly Thudd's purple button started to blink again. It popped open and the hologram of Uncle Al appeared. He was wearing a T-shirt with a picture of an iguana on it.

"Hey there!" said Uncle Al with a big smile. "Sorry it took so long to get your message."

"Hey, Uncle Al!" said Andrew.

"Hiya, Unkie!" said Thudd.

"We're up a stupid tree, Uncle Al," said Judy. "You've got to get us out of here!"

Uncle Al's eyebrows went up. "You guys are great climbers," he said. "I'm surprised you can't get down by yourselves. But I'll be right over. Where are you?"

When Uncle Al visited Andrew and Judy by using his Hologram Helper, he could hear them but not see them.

"In the Australian *rain forest,*" said Judy.

"Good golly, Miss Molly!" exclaimed Uncle Al. His eyebrows came together. "How did *that* happen?"

"It's a long story," said Andrew. "But—"

"It doesn't matter how we got here," Judy interrupted. "All that matters is getting out before we get eaten by beetles or birds or something."

"The Australian rain forest is a dangerous

place," said Uncle Al, "but you don't have to worry about beetles and birds."

"Um, that's not exactly true," said Andrew. "We, uh, got ourselves shrunk by the Goa Constrictor I built to shrink garbage. Now we're the size of small beetles."

"Albert Einstein on an egg sandwich!" exclaimed Uncle Al. "You *shrunk* yourselves again?" He shook his head. "I'll get the whole story later," he said. "But I need to leave right away so I can get to Australia tonight. Do you have any idea where you are?"

meep . . . "Northeast part of Australia," said Thudd.

"Ah!" said Uncle Al. "The Daintree Rain Forest. Let me think." He crossed his arms over his chest. "I have an idea," he said.

THUDD

TRAPPED!

Uncle Al rubbed his chin. "It would be very hard to find you in the middle of the rain forest," he said. "But a river runs through it. If you can find a way to travel down the river, it will carry you to a place where I *can* find you."

"Wowzers!" said Andrew. He pushed a hand into one of his pants pockets. "I have some Umbubble," he said. "We can use it to float down the river!"

Umbubble was a special bubble gum that Andrew had invented. You could blow it up so big that you could get inside it.

Judy frowned. "We're surrounded by trees

in this stupid jungle," she said. "We'll never be able to see where the river is."

"What kind of a tree are you in?" asked Uncle Al.

meep . . . "Strangler fig," said Thudd.

"Great!" said Uncle Al. "They're usually very tall. Climb to the top of the tree. You'll probably be able to see the river from there. Note the direction, climb down the tree, and hike to the river."

Judy groaned. "Climb up the tree! Climb down the tree! Hike to the river! There's dangerous stuff in these trees. And who knows what awful things are on the ground and in the river."

Uncle Al wasn't smiling now. "You guys have done things that no one else has ever done," he said. "You can do this. Keep your eyes open and be very careful."

"How will you find us on the river, Uncle Al?" asked Andrew.

"I have to talk fast," said Uncle Al. "The batteries on my Hologram Helper are running out. Listen closely.

"On the edge of the rain forest, there's a village," said Uncle Al. "You'll see the lights. The river is very narrow there. I'll string a fine net across the river and catch you."

"But how will you even know you caught us?" asked Judy. "We're so small, and it will be dark by then. You'll never find us."

meep . . . "Got idea, Unkie!" squeaked Thudd.

"What is it, Thudd?" asked Uncle Al.

meep . . . "Lotsa rain-forest stuff glow in dark," said Thudd. "Bugs, caterpillars, worms, mushrooms got bioluminescence. Mean 'living light.'"

A smile stretched across Uncle Al's face. "Brilliant, Thudd!" he said. His voice was beginning to sound far away. "Ghost mushrooms! They glow so brightly, you can read by their light. They're easy to find on the forest floor."

Uncle Al's voice was so soft that Andrew and Judy could barely hear him. His hologram was fading.

"Uncle Al, you're disappearing!" said Judy.

Uncle Al raised his eyebrows. His lips moved faster, but it sounded as though he were mumbling underwater.

"Uncle Al!" shouted Judy. "Come back!"

But with a pop and wiggle, he disappeared.

Andrew looked at Judy and shrugged. "Guess we'd better get climbing," he said.

Judy glanced up and shook her head. "The top of the tree is so high, we can't even see it," she said.

"It'll be easy to climb up," said Andrew. "The bark is rough. And we can grab on to the ferns and mosses."

Judy cocked her head. "And what about the weird things that want to eat us?" she said.

meep . . . "Peppermint smell keep some animals away . . . maybe," said Thudd.

Judy rolled her eyes. "*Thank* you, Thudd."

Andrew grabbed the stem of a fern frond, got a foothold in the tree bark, and began climbing.

"Come on!" he called down to Judy. "It's getting darker. It must be way past noon by now. We've got to meet Uncle Al tonight."

"Humph," Judy grumbled. But she grabbed a long gray strand of moss and started up.

Climbing was hard. Soon Andrew and Judy were huffing and puffing. Sweat dripped down their foreheads and into their eyes. Their arms and legs got scraped by the tree bark. They were too out of breath to talk.

A stream of green ants trickled down the tree. Andrew would have liked more of that fizzy, limy stuff, but there was no time for that.

meep . . . "Look!" squeaked Thudd, pointing up. "Top of the tree close, close, close!"

"Wowzers schnauzers!" cheered Andrew. "We can get there in half an hour!"

Judy stopped and pushed strands of hair away from her sweaty face. "I need a break," she said.

She crept from the tree trunk to a branch and flopped down on an orange fungus.

"Just for a couple of minutes," said Andrew, sitting down beside her.

Suddenly something dropped over them. A net!

7

EAT *THIS!*

"YAAAAAH!" hollered Judy.

"Holy moly!" said Andrew.

He tried to pull the net off. But the more he struggled, the more tangled he got.

Eek! squeaked Thudd. "Net-throwing spider! Spider weave net from spider silk. Watch for prey. Throw net on top of prey. Then spider bite prey with poison fangs! Gotta get out *fast, fast, fast!*"

"I'm *trying!*" said Judy, pulling at the spider silk. It stretched like chewing gum. The more they pulled, the more net there was to trap them.

"Noop! Noop! Noop!" squeaked Thudd. "Not pull web. Gotta *eat* web! Saliva in mouth break web!"

Judy's mouth dropped open and her eyes grew wide.

meep . . . *"EAT! EAT! EAT!"* screeched Thudd.

Andrew heard a rustle behind him. He spun around.

A leaf quivered. In the shadow under the leaf, Andrew spied a hairy head. Below its two enormous, round black eyes were two gigantic, hairy fangs.

"YAAARGH!" cried Andrew. His legs felt like pudding.

Andrew turned and began stuffing globs of spider net into his mouth. *Tastes kind of like milk,* he thought.

Judy was eating frantically, too. Her cheeks bulged with spiderweb.

Suddenly Andrew felt something brush

his back. The hairy brown fangs of the spider were rising up behind him!

Andrew froze. Judy grabbed his arm and shoved him through the hole they'd eaten in the net.

Broken strands of silk caught on their

clothes, but they ripped themselves away. They were free!

But the spider tore through its net. It was scuttling after them!

"Ack!" screamed Judy as a claw scratched her scalp.

They stumbled as fast as they could over the rough bark of the tree branch. Andrew looked frantically for a place to hide from the spider.

meep . . . "Look, Drewd!" Thudd squeaked. He was pointing to a group of tall, thick green towers sticking up from the branch.

Hanging down from one of the towers was a star-shaped, red-and-white-striped flower. It was as big as a person's foot.

Andrew and Judy ducked under ferns and mosses as they scrambled toward the strange-looking thing.

"Ugh!" said Judy breathlessly. "Something stinks!"

"Woofers!" said Andrew. "It's worse than when we got lost in the garbage! What *is* that thing?"

The closer they got to the strange plant, the worse the smell grew. The giant flower was covered with fuzzy red hairs—and lots of flies.

meep . . . "Called dead-horse plant," said Thudd. "Cuz flower stink like dead thing.

"Smell of dead-horse flower bring flies. Pollen from flower stick to flies. Flies carry pollen to other dead-horse flowers. Then flowers make seeds. Seeds make more baby dead-horse plants."

meep . . . "Hide under dead-horse plant," said Thudd.

One of the spider's clawed feet pricked Andrew's leg.

"YEOW!" hollered Andrew.

With a burst of energy, he flung himself between the green cactus-like columns of the dead-horse plant.

Suddenly the spider stopped. It scuttled to the monster flower. In a blur of speed, the fangs snatched a fly.

Judy shivered. "That could have been you—*or me!*" she whispered.

meep . . . "Spider busy eating fly," said Thudd. "Drewd and Oody gotta get out now. Gotta go up tree. Gotta find river."

Slowly, quietly, Andrew and Judy crawled

out from the green columns and away from the spider.

They reached the tree trunk and began climbing again.

Thudd pointed out the birds that flashed through the trees—screaming orange-and-green king parrots, black riflebirds that made a sound like a gunshot, and green catbirds that meowed.

These sounds were all part of the whistling, buzzing, cackling, screaming, screeching music of the rain forest.

meep . . . "Drewd and Oody near treetops now," Thudd said. "Called canopy of rain forest. Lotsa animals live in canopy. Lotsa light up here. Lotsa water from lotsa, lotsa rain. Canopy make shade for stuff that live underneath. Keep rain forest cool."

Andrew kept climbing. "We're higher than most of the other trees now," he said.

"So where's that stupid river?" said Judy.

Just then, Andrew thought he saw a sparkle of light through the leaves. He climbed quickly to get a clear view.

And then he saw it—a sliver of silvery river.

"Super-duper pooper-scooper!" Andrew yelled, creeping from the trunk to a branch. "The river! It's close!" he shouted to Judy, who was inches behind him.

As he looked down, Andrew glimpsed something that made the back of his neck prickle.

A few branches below, a coil of yellow-and-black stripes was beginning to unwind.

FASTEN YOUR SEAT BELTS . . .

Eek! squeaked Thudd. "Python snake!"

Judy's face went white.

"S-s-s-snake?" she stuttered.

"Get up here, Judy!" yelled Andrew. "There's a hole in the trunk. We can hide in it!"

In an instant, Judy scrambled up to where Andrew was.

Andrew pushed away strands of moss that covered the hole and crept inside. Judy followed him. At first it was too dark to see.

"We should be safe here," said Andrew.

"Wait a minute," said Judy. "You're the

one who told me that a snake's tongue can smell prey. And that they've got these little pits near their jaws that feel the heat from warm-blooded animals—*like us!* So just because it's dark in here doesn't mean a snake can't find us."

meep . . . "Oody and Drewd got peppermint smell," said Thudd. "Hide animal smell. Oody and Drewd small, small, small. Not got lotsa heat. Hard for snake to find, maybe."

Andrew thought he heard a soft grumble. He remembered the strange noises he had heard deep inside the tree trunk.

"There's something in here," he whispered to Judy.

As his eyes got used to the darkness, Andrew made out a shape. It was a creature the size of a chipmunk. It seemed to be asleep. Its ears were as big as bats' ears. Its eyes were closed. But Andrew could tell by its bulging lids that its eyes were enormous.

"It's so *cute!*" said Judy.

"But it would, uh, probably eat us if it were awake," said Andrew.

"Yoop! Yoop! Yoop!" said Thudd. "Called sugar glider. Live in treetops of rain forest. Eat bugs.

"Got flap of skin between front and back legs. When sugar glider jump from trees, stretch legs. Skin flap stretch like sail. Sugar glider glide from tree to tree.

"Sugar glider is marsupial like kangaroo. Female marsupial got pouch for baby. Look."

By the light of Thudd's face screen, Andrew could see a little slit where a belly button would be.

"Well, it's sleeping," said Judy. "We can hide from the snake and it won't even know we're here."

Eek! squeaked Thudd. "Sugar glider is snake candy! Sugar glider big enough for snake to smell, feel heat."

Andrew examined the opening of the hole. "I don't know if the hole is big enough for the snake to get in," he said.

"But it's sure going to try," said Judy.

For a moment, the only sound inside the hole was the sugar glider snoring.

"I have an idea," said Judy. "Andrew, go see where the snake is now."

Andrew peered over the edge of the hole. The snake was curling around the tree trunk. Andrew could see its thin black tongue flicking in and out of its mouth.

"It's coming up," said Andrew. "But it's moving slowly."

"Get into the pouch, Bug-Brain," said Judy.

"Huh?" said Andrew. "Snakes *eat* sugar gliders."

"Not if there aren't any sugar gliders to eat," said Judy. "We'll rumble around inside her pouch. If we're lucky, she'll wake up, scoot out of the hole, and glide away before the snake gets here.

"Come on," said Judy. "And be careful not to wake her up till we're ready."

"Wowzers!" said Andrew. "If this works, we save us *and* the sugar glider."

Andrew crept quickly to the middle of the furry sleeping body. He began wiggling his way into the pouch, feetfirst. It was like getting into bed with sheets tucked tightly under the mattress. Inside the pouch, it was hot and damp.

The sugar glider gave a little sigh and shifted in its sleep.

Judy had trouble getting in. She kicked Andrew in the head. She poked the sugar glider in the belly.

The sugar glider stirred. It shook itself. It rolled onto its feet and stuck its head out of the hole in the tree trunk.

Zih-zuh zih-zuh zih-zuh, it chattered.

meep . . . "Sugar glider afraid," Thudd said.

The sugar glider scurried onto the branch outside the hole and stood on its hind legs.

Sss sss sss, came a hiss. It sounded close. *Sssssss* . . .

A scaly yellow-and-black head rose above the branch. From the sugar glider's pouch, Andrew looked into the snake's black eyes. The snake's tongue darted so close, Andrew could have touched it.

Suddenly Andrew's stomach seemed to jump into his mouth. The sugar glider had flung itself from the branch. The skin between its front and back legs was stretched tight like a kite. They were sailing through the jungle!

The wind in Andrew's face made his eyes water. He looked down through the leafy layers of jungle speeding by and got dizzy.

The next instant, they jolted to a stop. The sugar glider had landed on the branch of

a small tree. She was licking her paws like a cat.

"Eeeuw!" shrieked Judy. "There's something wet and rubbery in here. It's squirming against my leg!"

Just then, a tiny, skinny dark tail poked out of the pouch between Andrew and Judy and disappeared. Then a little pink head no bigger than a baby's fingernail peeked out for an instant.

"Aaack!" Judy hollered. "It's a worm with a head!"

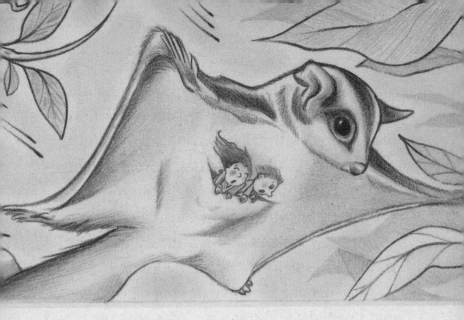

"Noop! Noop! Noop!" said Thudd. "Baby sugar glider. Called joey. Joey born small as grain of rice. Joey live in pouch, drink milk from mother for lotsa weeks."

Judy wrinkled her nose. "Let's get out of here," she said.

While the sugar glider was busy grooming herself, they snuck out of her pouch.

It was a short climb down to the rain-forest floor. The light was dim. The canopy of leaves blocked the sunlight.

Thick roots tangled over the wet ground. As far as Andrew could see, the forest floor was covered with fallen leaves, smashed fruit, and brightly colored funguses. Now and then, a damp leaf shuddered—as though something were moving underneath.

Andrew walked along a mossy root and sniffed the smells of the jungle floor.

Like wet dirt, he thought. *And rotten things and sweet, flowery stuff.*

The air was alive with buzzes and hisses and croaks. Judy poked Andrew's shoulder. "You saw the river, Bug-Brain," she said. "So which way is it?"

Andrew looked around. Then he pointed toward a thicket of vines with leaves as big as elephant ears. "Um, the river is that way . . . I think."

SAVED BY THE SMELL

Judy pushed her face next to Andrew's. "You'd better be right, Bug-Brain," she said. "Or else we're jungle chow."

The deep shadows of this place gave Andrew the spooks. "Let's get going," he said. "We have to get to the river."

"And we've got to find the ghost mushrooms before we get there," said Judy.

They began their trudge across the rainforest floor.

The jungle floor buzzed and chattered. Here and there, dead leaves twitched.

Kakaka kakaka . . . came a sound from behind them.

Andrew turned to see a slender flying in-sect, long as a pinkie finger, darting above a dark lump on the ground.

Then two legs—long, thin, dark, hairy legs—shot up from the lump. The lump was a fat, hairy spider. Its legs clawed the air, reaching for the insect. From leg to leg, the spider was the size of a dinner plate.

Andrew froze. "That spider looks as big as Godzilla!" he whispered.

meep . . . "Tarantula," said Thudd. "Called bird-eating spider! Eat lizards, snakes, frogs, birds!"

Kakaka kakaka kakaka . . .

"It's making weird sounds," said Judy.

meep . . . "Called barking spider, too," said Thudd.

"Spider in big fight with giant wasp called tarantula hawk. Cuz female wasp hunt taran-tulas.

"If wasp sting spider, spider not able to

move. Then wasp lay egg inside spider. When egg hatch, baby wasp eat spider alive."

"*Yuck!*" said Judy. "That is *soooo* disgusting!"

meep . . . "In lotsa places, *people* eat tarantulas. Taste like crab meat!"

"Neato mosquito!" said Andrew.

"*Aaaaack!*" Judy gagged.

With one of its front legs, the spider was scraping hairs off the front of its body. Then it flung them at the wasp!

"*Duck! Duck! Duck!*" squeaked Thudd. "Tarantula hair got lotsa poison!"

The fierce battle was scuffling closer to Andrew and Judy.

"Let's get out of here!" gasped Judy.

meep . . . "Hide behind gympie-gympie tree!" said Thudd.

He pointed to a small, pretty tree with heart-shaped leaves the size of pizzas.

"But no touch! Gympie-gympie tree got

hairs on leaves, hairs on trunk. Every hair is tiny glass needle filled with strong poison.

"If animal touch gympie-gympie tree, hairs dig into skin. Hurt! Hurt! Hurt! Even spider not touch gympie-gympie tree."

Andrew and Judy scurried behind the gympie-gympie tree. They watched as the tarantula and the wasp charged each other. At last, the tarantula scuttled under a thorny bush. The wasp flew off.

"Let's go," said Andrew.

Careful to stay away from its horrible hairs, Andrew and Judy crept away from the gympie-gympie tree. They continued their trek over the wet, slippery leaves.

The light was getting dimmer. They strained to see the glow of ghost mushrooms on the shadowy forest floor.

Suddenly Andrew felt something grab his ankles.

"Erf!" he cried.

The next instant, he was upside down!

Eek! squeaked Thudd, clinging to the edge of Andrew's pocket.

"Aaaack!" hollered Judy.

They were upside down and speeding away!

They were heading for a long black snout attached to a small head with beady black eyes! The animal's body was completely

covered with long, sharp brown quills.

"Yowzers!" cried Andrew.

"Noooooo!" cried Judy.

"Echidna!" squeaked Thudd. "Spiny ant-eater! Nose feel electric signals from living things. From ants, from bugs, from Drewd and Oody!"

Just as they reached the dark tunnel of the echidna's mouth, the tongue stopped reeling them in.

Snoof snoof, sniffed the echidna.

Judy shuddered. "We're going to be eaten by a pincushion with a head," she moaned.

Then, as fast as the echidna's tongue had reeled them in, it spun them out and shook them off.

Judy and Andrew landed in a brown slimy puddle. The echidna turned and waddled away.

"Cheese Louise!" shouted Judy. "We got lucky!"

"I wonder why it didn't eat us," said Andrew.

meep . . . "Drewd and Oody still smell like peppermint," said Thudd. "Maybe echidna not like peppermint."

Andrew and Judy wiped the slime off as best they could and trudged on.

As the day grew late, the colors of the rain forest faded to black and gray. The screeches and screams died away. Now the jungle chirped and chittered and whistled. The air felt like a cool velvet blanket against Andrew's skin.

Andrew stopped and sniffed the air. "I smell something fishy," he said. "We're getting close to the river."

Judy peered into the shadows. "I see lights!" she said.

THE BIGGEST PROBLEM IS GETTING SMALLER . . .

THUDD

meep . . . "Ghost mushrooms!" squeaked Thudd.

"I never thought I'd be so happy to see a fungus," said Judy.

They picked their way through the darkness toward the little lights.

The ghost mushrooms surrounded a huge tree trunk like a necklace. The cap at the top of each mushroom looked like a glowing, pale green parachute.

Judy stood under one of the mushrooms. "We're too small to break off chunks of these mushrooms," she said.

meep . . . "Cap of mushroom got lotsa thin, thin sheets underneath," said Thudd.

"Sheets called gills. Gills got tiny spores. Spores make baby mushrooms.

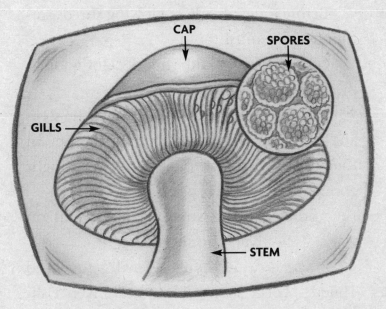

"Gotta climb up stem of mushroom, pull off gills."

Andrew and Judy shinnied up a mushroom stem. The gills were as thin as tissue paper. They were almost as close together as the pages of a book.

Andrew and Judy ripped off bits of the

soft, spongy gills and tossed them to the ground. Tiny round spores rained down like twinkling fairy powder.

Before long, a circle of glowing shreds surrounded the mushroom.

"Okey-dokey!" said Thudd. "Got enough pieces now."

Andrew and Judy climbed down the stem and gathered up the bits of mushroom in their arms. The mushroom heaps were bright enough to light their path.

Andrew spied a streak of moonlight on water. "The river!" he shouted.

meep . . . "Careful, Drewd!" squeaked Thudd. "Lotsa strange stuff near river. Fish-catching spiders! Toad that spray deadly poison!"

"*Thanks,* Thudd," said Judy.

At the riverbank, their feet sank in the squishy mud up to their ankles. They plodded along until they found a little pool of water at the edge of the river.

Andrew placed his pile of mushroom gills on a pebble. From a pants pocket, he pulled a small paper-wrapped square. The wrapper was printed with the word UMBUBBLE.

Andrew pulled off the paper, popped the blue square into his mouth, and chewed.

He blew a bubble as big as his head. Andrew kept blowing until the Umbubble was bigger than he was, till it was as big as a Ping-Pong ball.

"Whew!" Andrew sighed. He rolled the Umbubble onto a leaf.

"We'll stick the mushroom pieces on the inside so Uncle Al can see us," said Andrew.

Then Andrew rolled the Umbubble to the edge of the water. He found the small hole in the Umbubble where he had blown air into it. He shoved his head through the hole, then his shoulders, then the rest of him.

"Hand me all the mushroom pieces, Judy," he said. "And come on in."

Judy heaped the shreds in her arms and

shoved them through the hole. Then she pushed herself inside the Umbubble.

"Stick the pieces on quickly," said Andrew, "before the Umbubble dries and gets hard."

Andrew and Judy worked fast to cover the inside of the Umbubble with the glowing fragments.

When they were done, Andrew sealed the Umbubble by pulling the edges of the hole together. "It'll be ready in a few seconds," said Andrew.

Judy tapped the Umbubble. "Feels like plastic," she said.

"Now we get the Umbubble into the water," said Andrew. "Just walk inside it like a gerbil in a wheel."

They walked, and the glowing Umbubble rolled into the little pool.

Moonlit ripples of water pulled them away from the dark shapes on the shore. Soon the river current picked them up and raced them away.

All of a sudden, the Umbubble came to a stop.

"We must be caught on something," said Andrew.

He peered through a space between the mushroom pieces. The Umbubble had washed up against something—something big.

"Looks like a log," said Andrew. He squinted. *"A log with eyes!"*

meep . . . "Platypus!" said Thudd.

"A platypus!" said Andrew. "I've always wanted to see a platypus. But I always thought I'd be bigger than the platypus when I saw it."

"Platypus!" said Judy, trying to get a good view. "The bizarre-o mammal that has a beak like a duck and lays eggs."

meep . . . "Got beaver tail and webbed

feet," said Thudd. "Platypus beak feel electricity from animal muscles. Find prey same way as echidna."

"And we're right next to its beak," said Judy.

The Umbubble rolled over a wave. On the other side of it was a flying-saucer shape.

"What's that lump in the water?" asked Judy. "It's headed right at us."

Eek! squeaked Thudd. "Numbfish! Numbfish make electricity. Make big shock to catch prey!"

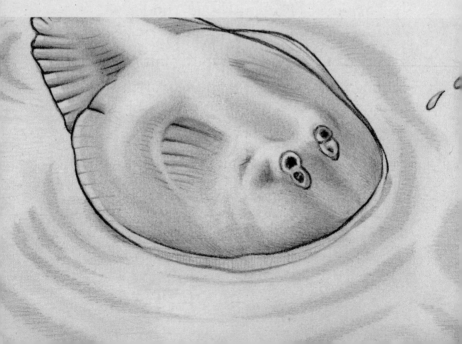

Suddenly Andrew's stomach lurched as the Umbubble flew up, spun around, and plopped back into the water.

A powerful tingle began in Andrew's toes. It jangled up to his head like lightning and pounded his skull like a hammer.

Black-and-white spirals twirled in front of his eyes. Then everything went completely dark.

Andrew was having a dream about octopuses battling platypuses when he heard a little voice.

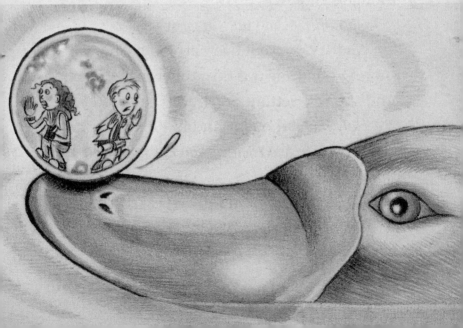

meep . . . "Wake up, Drewd," squeaked Thudd.

Andrew rubbed his eyes. "Huh? Wha?" he mumbled sleepily.

meep . . . "Umbubble get shock from numbfish," said Thudd. "Drewd been sleeping long time."

Andrew's head wasn't pounding anymore and the spirals were gone, but he felt a little dizzy.

Why does the top of the Umbubble look so far away? And why is it getting farther away? thought Andrew.

Ga-nufff . . . ga-nufff . . . gnewww . . .

Andrew looked over at Judy. She was snoring—and she was tiny, tinier than before. And she was getting tinier every second.

Holy moly! thought Andrew. *It must be the electricity. The electricity from the numbfish is shrinking us smaller!*

meep . . . "Look, Drewd!" squeaked Thudd. "Lights of village!"

Indeed, as Andrew peered through the Umbubble, he saw lights on the bank of the river. He saw the dark outline of a boat—and the familiar shape of Uncle Al!

The Umbubble whammed against something and stopped suddenly. The jolt sent Andrew and Judy flying through the Umbubble. Andrew landed against Judy.

"Super-duper pooper-scooper!" said Andrew. "We're caught in Uncle Al's net!"

"Wake up, Judy! Uncle Al's here! We're getting rescued!"

But Judy just rolled over and kept on snoring—and getting smaller.

The boat was almost on top of the Umbubble now.

The next moment, the Umbubble swooped into the air. Between the mushroom pieces, Andrew saw Uncle Al's giant fingers.

Something tapped the Umbubble.

Ping!

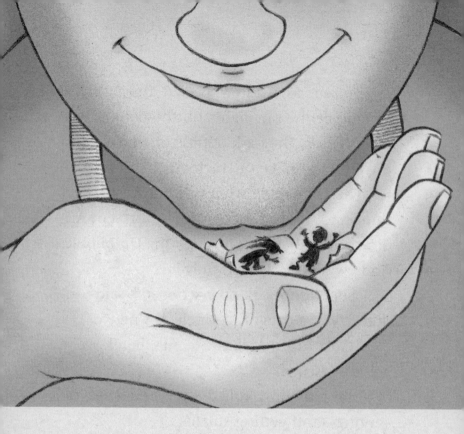

It cracked. Andrew, Judy, and Thudd fell onto Uncle Al's palm and bounced onto his wrist.

Uncle Al beamed a flashlight on his open hand. His smiling face glowed like a full moon.

"Super-duper pooper scooper!" cheered Andrew. "We're *safe*!"

TO BE CONTINUED IN ANDREW, JUDY, AND THUDD'S

NEXT EXCITING ADVENTURE:

ANDREW LOST
IN UNCLE AL

In stores July 2007

THUDD

TRUE STUFF

Thudd wanted to tell you more about carnivorous plants and platypuses, but he was busy keeping Andrew and Judy from being gulped by a python and stung by a gympie-gympie tree. Here's what he wanted to say:

• Most plants use their roots to take up all the food they need from the soil. But rain-forest soil doesn't have much food. That's why some rain-forest plants catch insects and some other small animals—they need the extra nutrition.

• Rhinoceros beetles might be the strongest animals on earth. One rhinoceros beetle could carry 800 other rhinoceros beetles on its back! A human who was as strong as a rhinoceros beetle could carry seventy cars!

• Australia has ten thousand kinds of spiders, more than any other place in the world. And new kinds are being discovered all the time. Australia also takes the prize for spiders with the strongest venom.

• There are different kinds of rain forests. Rain forests in warm areas near the equator are called tropical rain forests or jungles. These are what we think of when we hear the words *rain forest.*

There are a few rain forests in cooler areas, too. These are called temperate rain forests.

The plants and animals in the two kinds of rain forests are quite different. In tropical rain forests, trees usually have large, broad leaves to capture as much sunlight as they can. In temperate rain forests, most of the trees have needles like pine trees. There are more different kinds of plants and animals in tropical rain forests.

But all rain forests get lots of rain—at least

a hundred inches of rain each year. (A six-foot-tall person is seventy-two inches high.) Some rain forests get *400* inches of rain in a year!

• Tropical rain forests have layers. The layer created by the treetops is called the canopy. This layer covers the rain forest like an umbrella. The canopy gets most of the sunlight, and most of the rain-forest animals live there. The canopy keeps the rain forest cool.

Some very tall trees, like the one that Andrew and Judy climb, stick up through the canopy. These especially tall trees make up the emergent layer of the rain forest.

The area between the canopy and the forest floor is called the understory. It gets much less light. Bushes and ferns and young trees are found there.

The forest floor gets only a tiny amount of light. Whatever falls to the ground—dead leaves, dead animals, poop—is quickly eaten by insects and other animals. These things disappear so fast that they never release their nutrients back into the soil. That's one reason why the soil doesn't contain much food for plants. Another reason is that the huge amounts of rain wash away the nutrients in the soil.

• Platypuses may be the strangest animals in the world. A platypus is a furry mammal with a flat bill like a duck, webbed feet, and a wide, flat tail that stores fat for the winter. And they lay eggs! Platypuses and echidnas are the only mammals that lay eggs.

Platypus eggs are sticky—they stick to the fur on their mother's belly. When the eggs hatch, the baby platypuses hang on to their mother's belly fur and drink milk.

The only places where you can find platypuses and echidnas in the wild are Australia and some nearby islands.

• When scientists first saw a platypus that was stuffed and sent back to England, they didn't believe it was a real animal. They tried to find stitches to prove that it was sewn together from the parts of many different animals!

WHERE TO FIND MORE TRUE STUFF

Would you like to find out more about weird and wonderful rain forests? Here are some books you might enjoy:

• *Afternoon on the Amazon* by Mary Pope Osborne (New York: Random House Books for Young Readers, 1995). All rain forests are different. Read this book if you'd like an adventure that includes the piranhas, jaguars, and flesh-eating ants of the South American rain forest.

• *Rain Forests* by Will Osborne and Mary Pope Osborne (New York: Random House Books for Young Readers, 2001). This is the nonfiction companion book to *Afternoon on the Amazon.* It's full of great facts about the rain forest and tips for even more research.

• *One Day in the Tropical Rain Forest* by Jean Craighead George (New York: HarperTrophy, 1995). Rain forests are mysterious places that are home to many plants and animals that haven't been discovered. Yet large areas of rain forests are destroyed every year. This book tells the story of how one boy helped save his rain forest and why it's worth saving.

• *One Small Square: Tropical Rain Forest* by Donald M. Silver (New York: McGraw-Hill, 1998). If you want to see great pictures of what lives in every layer of the rain forest, look for this book. You'll also find amazing facts, fun activities, and easy experiments.

• *Australian Animals* by Caroline Arnold (New York: HarperCollins, 2000). Did you know that penguins live in Australia? Can you imagine what a thorny devil looks like? And what is a quoll? In this book, you'll find great pictures and facts about some absolutely amazing Australian animals.

• *Platypus* by Joan Short, Jack Green, and Bettina Bird (New York: Mondo Publishing, 1997). You've got to see what a platypus looks like! You'll also learn about how they live along the riverbanks in Australia.

• *National Geographic: Really Wild Animals— Totally Tropical Rain Forest* (Washington, D.C.: National Geographic Society, 1994). If you can't hop a plane and visit a rain forest right now, get your hands on this videotape!

Turn the page
for a sneak peek at
Andrew, Judy, and Thudd's
next exciting adventure—

ANDREW LOST
IN UNCLE AL

Available July 2007

1 NYEEEEEEEEEE . . .

Andrew Dubble, smaller than a speck of dust, flopped onto his Uncle Al's wrist.

Ga-nufff . . . ga-nufff . . . ga-newww . . . Judy snored.

With one hand, Andrew clutched the collar of Judy's jacket to keep her from falling off Uncle Al's wrist. With his other hand, Andrew clung to a hair.

Nyeeeeeeeee . . .

The sound was close by. *A mosquito,* thought Andrew.

NYEEEEEEEEEE . . .

Then Andrew made out what looked like the hairy bud of a flower with a long stem.

At the other end of the stem was a horrible face. Two large black eyes covered most of it like a helmet. Hairy antennas stuck out from under the eyes.

The bud-shaped thing was zooming down toward Andrew and Judy. Suddenly it opened and slammed down over them.

Eek! squeaked Thudd. "Mosquito snout! Called proboscis."

Andrew and Judy were squashed between two walls with razor-sharp edges!

"Mosquito gonna bite!" squeaked Thudd.

"Androoooo?" Judy said sleepily.

"Jeepers creepers!" said Andrew. "You've been asleep for a long time!"

Judy rubbed her eyes. "Where are we?" she asked. "Where's Uncle Al?"

Before Andrew could answer, the blades inside the snout started moving. They were sawing into Uncle Al's skin!

Andrew sniffed a coppery smell. *Blood!* he thought.

Eek! . . . "Mosquito snout gonna push Drew and Oody inside Uncle Al!" squeaked Thudd. "Drewd got Schnozzle?"

Andrew pushed a hand into his pants pocket. He pulled out two pairs of black goggles with noses attached and mustaches underneath. He handed one pair to Judy.

"Put on the Schnozzle!" said Andrew.

"This isn't *Halloween!*" Judy yelled.

meep . . . "Quick! Quick! Quick!" said Thudd.

The blades of the proboscis were sawing a hole in Uncle Al's skin. Andrew and Judy were on the very edge. A blade caught on Andrew's jacket and pulled him into the hole.

"Yowzers!" hollered Andrew.

"Aaaaaack!" yelled Judy, tumbling in after.

Just as Andrew was hooking the earpieces of the Schnozzle behind his ears, a blasting spray drove him down and down. Before he could scream, Andrew disappeared under Uncle Al's skin.

Bring magic into your life with these enchanting books!

Magic Tree House® series
by Mary Pope Osborne

The Magic Elements Quartet
by Mallory Loehr
Water Wishes
Earth Magic
Wind Spell
Fire Dreams

Dragons
by Lucille Recht Penner

Fox Eyes
by Mordicai Gerstein

King Arthur's Courage
by Stephanie Spinner

The Magic of Merlin
by Stephanie Spinner

Unicorns
by Lucille Recht Penner